Evil Eye Beagle

Funny
Sport Stories

by

Harrison Powers

Watermill Press

Illustrations by Jim Odbert

ISBN 0-89375-703-9

Contents

Evil Eye Beagle

I suppose you'd say that no dog can lay a whammy on a hockey team. Well, Beagle could.

A whammy, in case you didn't know, comes from the old Evil Eye. You're walking down the street, for instance. A flowerpot falls on your head. Chances are, somebody laid a whammy on you. If a guy takes your wallet while

I found Beagle in an alley.

you're lying there—that's a double whammy. I don't even like to think about a triple whammy.

I found Beagle in an alley. He was cold and hungry. Since I have a soft spot in my heart for hungry mutts, I took him home. We didn't eat fancy, but we ate well. Beagle liked that.

I found out that Beagle had an Evil Eye because of what happened to Donny the Shark. I owed Donny a couple of hundred bucks. And, since I had missed a payment or two, he stopped by to see me.

"You wouldn't like to have an unlucky accident, would you?" Donny said.

I shook my head.

"Then you will please not keep me waiting." Donny was leaning against the stair railing. He was blowing dust from his fingernails at the time.

I could see Beagle didn't like Donny. He growled and his eyes bugged out of his head. As soon as he did that, the stair rail broke.

"He can do a whammy," I said to myself as I called for an ambulance.

Now, I happen to like hockey. In fact, I'm a real hockey nut. In fifteen years, I've never missed a home game of the Greenville Seals.

Normally they are a good team. Normally they are good enough not to get caught roughing or tripping. They can score like crazy when they don't get caught.

But this year they couldn't get anything past the ref. This means they always have guys in the penalty box. This means they are always short-handed. And, if you get my meaning, they are always getting creamed.

So, when I saw what Beagle could do, I took him to a game. I got a good seat right at rink-side. Then I showed Beagle which one was the referee.

"That one," I said and pointed. "He is strictly no good."

Beagle growled and his eyes bugged. Right away the ref fell down. "This," I said, "is going to be a good night."

When the Seals skated onto the ice, I yelled like crazy. "These are the good guys," I said to Beagle. I could see he knew. He jumped up and down and licked my face.

"And these are the bums," I said when the Hawks came on.

Beagle growled. "Cut it out," I said to him. "We don't cheat. We only do a whammy on the referee. And just a small one. We don't want anybody hurt."

Things were going well in the first period. It was 6–0 Seals, and the referee had hurt his neck. It put his timing off.

*His skate blade broke, and he slid into
the goalie.*

So the Seals could get away with most anything. I could see Beagle was enjoying hockey. He was getting more and more excited.

In the second period, the ref had a hard time skating. He had twisted his knee or something. The score was now 11-0 Seals.

Then a forward for the Hawks got hurt. His skate blade broke, and he slid into the goalie. It took a while to get them out of the net.

This had me worried. "Cut it out, Beagle," I said. "I told you we cannot cheat."

But Beagle now had a wild look in his eye. I could see he was out of control. It got worse as the game went on.

Five minutes into the third period the score was 32-0. The Hawks only had two men left who could skate. I never saw a dog so excited.

The Bloomville Blues got beaten.

"Enough!" I yelled. And I started to drag Beagle to the exit.

I had my back to the rink, so I didn't see it happen. But I knew something was wrong from the way people were acting. Beagle had thrown a triple whammy. *He melted the ice!* I can tell you I got out of there fast.

"No more hockey for you," I told Beagle. "You are not a good sport."

I never did see a dog feel so bad. That night he ran away. That was five years ago. I haven't seen Beagle since.

But I read just the other day that the Bloomville Blues got beaten 48-0. And the scoreboard had fallen down. So maybe Beagle is alive and well and living somewhere as a devoted hockey fan.

The Ledyard Losers

Jam looked at her players. She wondered if she had made a mistake. They sure looked like a bunch of losers.

Funky Finley was dropping balls like you wouldn't believe. But, compared to Biddy Barry, he was a star outfielder. Biddy said looking up gave her a stiff neck. So she would never try to catch a pop-up fly till it was right in front of her. By that time it was too late. She hadn't caught one yet.

Louie Ledyard was pitching. At least, he was *trying* to pitch. There was only one guy he could strike out — Mush Mankowski. Mush couldn't hit a baseball with a tennis racket.

Jam Hurley was coach, captain, and she played first base. The reason she played first base was that she had a tee shirt with a big target painted on it. This gave Ikey Roe over on third something to aim at. Jam was coach and captain because the whole thing was her idea. She was beginning to feel sorry about that. They were having the worst practice ever.

It all started when Mike's Burger Bar put together a team to play sandlot ball. Jam really wanted to be on that team. Mike bought them white uniforms with green lettering. The players' names were on the back, over the number. On the front it said "Mike's Burger Bar." And under that was a hamburger and a tall glass of soda with bubbles coming out of it.

"First of all," Mike said, "we don't want any girls on the team. They could get hurt. Second, my team is called 'The Stingaroos.' Whoever heard of a girl stingaroo? You've got to be first class to be a stingaroo."

Jam was getting madder by the minute. "OK, Mike, my friend," she said. "Are you a betting man?"

"Depends on the bet," Mike said.

"I'll bet a hundred bucks I can beat your Stinkaroos."

"It's Stingaroos," Mike said. "Besides, you don't have $100."

"Yes I do," Jam said. She pulled a bank book from her pocket and showed it to Mike.

"OK, wise guy," said Mike. "And just what will you beat my Stingaroos

Louie Ledyard's father owned a drugstore.

with—the New York Yankees?" Mike thought this was very funny. He laughed so hard he choked.

"The Loopers can beat them," Jam lied. "They're another team that wants me to be captain. They hit nothing but long looping home runs. That's why they're called the Loopers."

"OK," Mike said. "You've got a bet. One month to get ready. Right?"

"Right!" Jam agreed. And right away she felt she had put her foot in it. There were no Loopers. There was no team of any kind.

So first thing she did was see Louie Ledyard. His father owned a drugstore. And Louie owed Jam a couple of favors.

"What do I need with a baseball team?" Louie's father said.

"It's good for business, Pop," Louie said. "And besides, I owe this girl a favor."

The Ledyard Loopers were born. Louie's father got the uniforms. They were red with yellow numbers. Under the number on the front was an aspirin bottle. On the back it said "Ledyard's — We Deliver."

Now it was Tuesday. The game would be on Saturday. Things couldn't have been worse. Mike came by with the Stingaroo captain to watch the Loopers practice. He laughed so hard he started choking again.

"What's so funny?" asked Mr. Ledyard. He wanted to know why somebody was laughing at his team.

"Look!" was all Mike could say before he started choking again.

Louie pitched to Funky Finley. It went over Funky's head. Funky swung at it anyhow and missed. The catcher couldn't reach the ball, so she threw her glove at it.

The catcher couldn't reach the ball.

"What's funny?" asked Mr. Ledyard again. "That's my baseball team. And they're bad for business. I've got to do something."

"Maybe do a miracle," Mike said. He loved his own jokes. "Or maybe magic. Make them disappear. The Ledyard *Losers*." This was too much for Mike. He laughed so hard the captain of the Stingaroos had to hold him up.

This gave Mr. Ledyard an idea. "You want magic? You'll get magic, Mr. Smart Guy. You just bring your Stinkaroos on Saturday. I'll give them magic."

Mr. Ledyard went to his drugstore. He fooled around in back for a while. When he came out he had a large bottle of pills. He took these to his team. "Jam," he said, "bring those jokers over here."

"These," said Mr. Ledyard to the team, "are magic pills. They were given to me by Professor Hinkle from Harvard. He got them from an old medicine man. If you take a pill it makes you strong as an ox. It makes you smart as a fox. It makes you winners instead of losers. Now take."

Jam was afraid of the strange-looking pills. So was Biddy. "I'm not taking any pills," Biddy said.

"Take!" said Mr. Ledyard. "It's good for your stiff neck."

"If my Pop says they're magic, then they're magic," Louie said. "He's the best druggist in town. Ask him. He'll tell you."

"That's right," Mr. Ledyard agreed. "I'm the greatest. Now take. If you don't take the pills, I take back the uniforms. You can play naked for all I care."

Louie was the first to take one.

Then Jam took one. Then Mush Mankowski took one, and the others did, too. Finally, Biddy Barry took hers and that was all of them. Then a strange thing happened.

After a while Louie found home plate when he pitched. Mush Mankowski actually hit a ball. And Biddy looked up and caught it. Jam couldn't believe her eyes. Biddy whipped the ball to Ikey at third. Ikey threw to Jam at first.

"Hey, hey, that's the way," hollered Jam.

"Give me another pill," Biddy hollered from center field.

On the day of the game Mr. Ledyard sent a case of soda pop to the Stingaroos. It was to show good will he said. He gave his own team bottled water and more magic pills. The Stingaroos finished the case of pop. Mr. Ledyard sent them another.

"See that soda pop they're drinking?" asked a little boy. He was sitting next to Mike. His name was Bobby Ledyard. Bobby was Louie's little brother.

Mike said, "Yeah, I see it. So what?"

"My father makes it himself," Bobby said. "I'm Bobby Ledyard."

"Again, so what?" Mike said.

"So I saw my father put pills in the soda."

"You saw what?" Mike screamed.

"He put pills in the soda." Bobby looked very serious.

Mike ran down on the field. "Don't drink the soda. It's been poisoned. Help! Police!"

The game stopped. Mr. Ledyard ran over. "What's the matter? Who's poisoned?" he asked.

"You poisoned my team," Mike screamed at him. "Your kid said so."

"Who? Bobby? He watches too much TV," Mr. Ledyard said. "Hey, are you trying to call off the game?"

Mike looked sheepish and went back to his seat.

Mr. Ledyard gave Bobby a dollar for being good and doing as he was told.

The Ledyard Loopers had been playing pretty well up to that point. But the Stingaroos were ahead 15 to 10. Then something funny happened. The captain of the Stingaroos got sick and threw up. Then the catcher got sick. Pretty soon there were Stingaroos throwing up all over the place.

Needless to say, you can't play much baseball when you're that sick. On the other hand, the Loopers were taking their pills and feeling great. They won the game 27 to 15.

Mike said his team had been poisoned. He had the soda pop tested.

"Just plain orange soda," is what

the report said.

Jam started wondering. She asked Mr. Ledyard, "Honest, Mr. Ledyard, what's in our magic pills?"

"Nothing so terrible." It was the first time Jam had seen Mr. Ledyard smile. "A little sugar. A little orange flavor."

"But...but...but...but," Jam couldn't get the words out.

"But they made you winners," said Mr. Ledyard. "So what's so terrible?"

"And what was in the poison soda pop?" Jam asked.

Mr. Ledyard smiled again. "The same thing. Sugar, a little orange flavor, and soda water."

"So how come the same gloop that made us winners made them sick?" Jam wanted to know.

By this time Mr. Ledyard was laughing so hard he couldn't talk too well. "A thing isn't always what it is,"

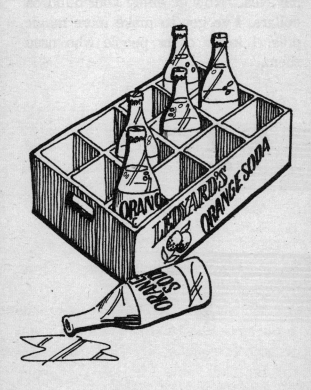

The poison soda pop.

he wheezed. "Sometimes it's what you think it is." He wiped happy tears from his eyes. "Now go enjoy your hundred dollars. I've got to make more magic pills. I know other people who need them."

The Borzhomi Nose

My mother has only been in the United States for a few months. She has lived all her life in a small mountain town in Georgia. Not Georgia, U.S.A. My mother is from the Georgia that's in Russia.

We were separated when I was very young. The details aren't important. But I grew up in the States while my mother remained in Russia. Now that she is here with me, I feel she should enjoy all the good things she has missed. And to my mind, the main thing is baseball.

I have been a baseball fan all my life. I love the game. *Baseball,* I said to myself, *will really show Mama what America is like.*

When I told her I would take her to a game, she seemed pleased.

"I like games," she said.

"Good. Nothing is too good for my Mama." I kissed her cheek. "I got box seats."

She seemed disappointed.

"What's the matter, Mama?" I asked.

"It's nothing," she said. "It's just I'm not so young anymore. I'm afraid I couldn't sit on a box."

Then her face lit up. She had an idea. "We could bring folding chairs from the porch," she said.

I explained the seats would be good enough. A little hard maybe, but all right.

When we got there, Mama was pleased with the crowds and the noise. She held tightly to my arm. In her free hand, she carried a large bag. *Her purse,* I told myself, *won't do for America.* I decided to buy her a new one.

We settled in our seats. Mama asked, "Would you like something to eat?" She opened the huge bag. It wasn't her purse after all. It turned out to be a traveling refrigerator.

The bag contained a two-foot salami, two kinds of bread, three tomatoes, six boiled eggs, a head of lettuce, and a large bottle of apple cider. There was

31

mustard, relish, ketchup, and horse-radish.

"I had a pie," she said sadly. "It wouldn't fit. We can have it when we get home. We'll probably be hungry."

"But Mama," I said. "I wanted to buy you the food here. They have hot dogs, popcorn, potato chips, soda, everything."

"They have salami and good black bread? Tomatoes?"

I had to admit they didn't.

"So eat and enjoy it," she said. She turned to the man beside her. "Hey mister. You want a salami sandwich?"

By the time Mama finished making sandwiches it was the end of the third inning. Everybody had salami and apple cider. We were getting dirty looks from the guy selling hot dogs. A woman behind me asked for more mustard.

Bruce Collins opened the fourth inning with a home run. The crowd was on its feet cheering. Mama put down her groceries and stood up to see.

"What is it?" she asked.

"A home run, Mama. The batter just made a home run." I was all excited.

"So why is there such a fuss if he had to run home a minute?" She looked puzzled. Then she saw something of greater interest.

"That man over there," she said. "Look at his nose."

I looked where she was pointing. It was the Eagles' manager. He had a large nose. But it was nothing special that I could see.

"It's a Borzhomi nose," Mama said.

"What," I wanted to know, "is a Borzhomi nose?"

Mama clicked her tongue. She

"It's a Borzhomi nose."

couldn't understand how I could ask such a stupid question. "Borzhomi is a town in Georgia," she explained. "It's not far from our home in Gori. Almost everybody is related there. And almost everybody has the same nose. It's a Borzhomi nose," she repeated.

It was the sixth inning. Morley Watts doubled. The next man walked. Foster Elson was up. A solid hit could put us ahead.

"Excuse me," Mama said. She got up as if to leave.

"Where are you going?" I asked her. "The game is just getting good."

"They have been doing the same thing for an hour," she said. "If I miss a few minutes it won't hurt. I have to find out if that man is from Borzhomi."

The man wasn't from Borzhomi. He was from Oakland. His father was from Borzhomi. How Mama got onto the playing field I don't know. But the

Eagles' manager seemed to like talking to her. And he seemed to be enjoying his salami sandwich.

"I told you it was a Borzhomi nose," she said on the way home. I didn't answer. The day had been a failure for me. I figured it was a mistake to expect Mama to like baseball.

Then Mama said, "Those Eagles are Number One. Maybe we'll beat the bums next time. You want an egg, Joseph? I got an egg left over."

The Great Gert

At one time, there were seven towns in the Sheebang River Valley. Each town had a football team. All the folks up and down the river loved the game. They were poor folks, though. They could not afford big teams.

Each team had exactly 11 players. There was no offense and defense. There weren't even any substitutes like

there are today. And the players got
ten dollars each whenever they played
a game. That was all. So when they
weren't playing, these football heroes
had other jobs. Some were farmers.
Some were coal miners. Others drove
trucks, worked in factories, or had
other ordinary jobs. But these people
weren't ordinary. They were special.
They were special because they played
football.

Women in the Sheebang Valley
loved football as much as the men. But,
of course, they weren't allowed to play
on the teams. Their fathers and hus-
bands were afraid they'd get hurt. So,
most women were satisfied to watch
and cheer.

Gert Mazurski was different. She
couldn't keep her hands off a football.
When training started in early summer
she was there. She never missed a
single practice of the Irontown In-

dians. If nothing else, she would run after stray balls for the team. Sometimes they let her be water girl. And, little by little, the men got used to having her around.

What no one knew was that Gert practiced secretly. She had a bull's-eye on her father's barn. This was her passing target. She got so she could hit it from 50 yards. She practiced kicking over the limb of a tree. She even made a dummy for blocking and tackling. What she did was stuff a scarecrow with 250 pounds of sand.

After a while, the men noticed how well she could throw a football. Then once, as a joke, she tackled Big Bill McGunn. He didn't come to for an hour. He said later it was because she sneaked up on him.

Anyhow, they started letting her fill in if someone missed practice. Once, Rifle Reese, the quarterback, wanted

She had a bull's-eye on her father's barn.

her to play in a game. That was when Belly Barnes got hurt. There were no substitutes, remember. That meant the Indians only had ten men to play with.

But Mr. Hindsite, the referee, said no. She might get hurt. And besides, it wasn't ladylike. The Indians lost that time, and Gert was really mad. "We could have won that game," she groaned. Rifle Reese agreed with Gert, but there was nothing he could do.

Then came the time when the Indians made it to the play-offs. Once again they were short a man. And Rifle Reese knew they couldn't beat the Pinehurst Reds short-handed. Mr. Hindsite stood firm, however. No woman would play while he was referee. So the Indians started off with only ten men.

The championship game wasn't four minutes old when the worst happened. Rifle Reese got hurt. Now there were only nine players for the Indians. And there wasn't a passer among them.

Rifle Reese pleaded with Mr. Hindsite. "Please let Gert play. She can pass as well as I can. And she can tackle as well as any man."

Mr. Hindsite shook his head. But then the Irontown fans started shouting and hooting.

"It isn't fair," Mr. Steele declared. "It isn't fair playing eleven against nine. If Reese says Gert can play, I say let her!" Mr. Steele was the Irontown mill owner. During the week he was Mr. Hindsite's boss. Hindsite had to give in.

Gert had to make herself a uniform fast. So she padded up a pair of her father's overalls. Then she pulled an Irontown jersey over that. The helmet was a bit of a problem. In those days, women piled their hair up. No helmet

"It isn't fair!"

would fit over her big hairdo. Finally, Gert undid her hair and let it fall free to her waist. Then she put on Rifle Reese's helmet.

She looked a sight and she knew it. But she was playing real football at last. And in a championship game at that!

"Don't hurt the little lady—much." That was Tunnel Turner, the Reds' tackle.

"When do we serve tea, boys?" Killer Quincy, the center, wanted to know.

"Watch out, you don't step on her hair." That was Bull Baker, fullback for the Reds.

The Reds had the ball. Gert figured she better put an end to the nonsense right off.

Bull Baker took a hand-off. With good blocking, he plunged through tackle. Then he came face to face with Gert.

"Watch out girlie," he sneered. "I'm on my way to a touchdown."

Bull stuck out his arm to shove Gert aside. She grabbed his wrist and held on. Then she swung him like a hammer. When he hit the ground they could hear the thud all the way back to Pinehurst. Bull smiled and swore it didn't hurt. But he walked funny for a long time after that.

Then Pinehurst set up for a pass play. Gink Garvey took the snap and faded back. Gert was after him in a flash. Tunnel Taylor braced himself to block her. Next thing he knew he was sitting on top of Gink. Gink dropped the ball and Gert recovered.

For the rest of the day Gert passed and Gert caught passes. Gert plugged holes when the line didn't hold. Gert ran

90 yards for a touchdown with her hair streaming out behind her. And so it went.

The Irontown fans went crazy. Bull Baker looked like he wanted to cry from the pain and shame. When the game was over he quit football forever. And women all up and down the valley started playing football. They did pretty well, too.

But it turned out the Sheebang Valley league was way ahead of its time. That's why the only woman to become famous in football was Gert. There's a statue of her that overlooks the Sheebang River. On the bottom it says simply:

THE GREAT GERT MAZURSKI
She Beat Them All

In other words, she won the whole Sheebang.

Why They Quit Playing Checkers in Stark Park

Why did they quit playing checkers in Stark Park? I can tell you why in one word. Barney! That's why.

Barney beat everyone around. He even beat Frank Stubbs. Frank was champion for ten years. And when he wasn't playing he was bothering who-

*He came to the park every day with
Charlie Simms.*

ever *was* playing. Barney was always hanging around and telling us how we should play.

If you know anybody like this, you know what a pain in the neck Barney was. He was a champ at checkers. And he was a champ at annoying everyone. You'd make a move. He'd make you take it back. You'd jump one way. He'd want another way. You'd want to make a king. He'd say *no, wait*.

The trouble is, he was always right. If Barney told you how to play, you'd win. If he told the other guy how to play, you'd lose. It never failed. So when Barney was around there was no use playing. You always knew who would win.

At first we thought it was cute. Barney was very young. He was only four years old and kind of shy. He came to the park every day with Charlie Simms. He'd walk up holding Charlie's hand. We'd all say, "Hi, Barney."

Then, without saying a word, Barney would climb up on the bench. He'd be ready to play. If someone else was playing, he'd be a pain in the neck till it was his turn.

Barney had a way of leaning forward when he sat. It kind of made you smile to see it. Then he'd scratch his head. When he started humming to himself he was ready to play.

He moved the checkers very carefully. He'd stick out one of his long fingers and push it. It was like he was playing shuffleboard or something. When he could make a jump he'd get all excited. He would bounce up and down and go *"ooo-ooo-ooo"* or something like that.

That seemed cute, too, at first. But it just meant you were losing again. So, after Barney won the championship, we had all had enough. We got together

Barney fell in love.

and took a vote. The vote was he couldn't play anymore. Charlie Simms was the only one who voted for Barney.

But, as I said, it got worse after that. Barney just hung around and bothered everyone. So, after a while, people quit playing. Then they quit coming to the park.

We should have been more patient. Soon after, Barney lost interest in checkers. The reason was that Barney fell in love. He would go to see Myrtle every day. He had no time for checkers or anything else. He would sit for hours with a silly smile on his face and watch that lady chimpanzee. And she would sit in her cage and smile back.

Maybe I should have told you right off. Barney was a chimpanzee, too. Why do you think we hated it so much when he beat us?

The Legend of Hootin' Holler

You might not find it on the map. And there isn't even a sign for it on the highway. But Hooting Hollow, Kentucky, is important to the people who live there. And all the folks around call it Hootin' Holler.

Nothing much happens in Hootin' Holler. But once a year they have a motorcycle race. The race was started back in 1922 by a fellow named Mac Adam. Most people just called him Big Mac.

Big Mac was the first in the valley to own a motorcycle. It was one of those big bikes. It came all the way from Springfield, Massachusetts.

There was nothing Mac liked to do better than ride that bike. Trouble was, he had no one to ride with. That's why he advertised for a race.

Only one fellow answered though. And he came all the way over from Tims Ford. Even so, it turned out they had the best bike race anybody ever had. It lasted almost four hours. Big Mac had set up the course himself.

It went five miles down the valley along Marsh Creek. Then it climbed up Lizard Mountain to the top. It went along the ridge from there. Then it dropped down through Suicide Gulch.

It was 16 miles in all. And they were supposed to go around ten times.

Big Mac was winning until the last lap. Then he lost control at Suicide Gulch. He hit a rock, flipped, and fell 150 feet into the gorge. The fall killed him, deader than a snake.

You might think that was the end of racing in Hootin' Holler. But it wasn't. There's been a race every year since, in honor of Big Mac. And every year a funny thing happens. The night before the race, the ghost of Big Mac appears. He doesn't float around or anything like that. He comes to one of the racers in a dream. And that person always wins.

Well, one year he came to Lu King. Actually, Lu shouldn't even have been in the race. She had entered for her brother Joe. Joe King had mashed his hand in a tractor.

"Don't do it, Lu," Joe said. "You haven't even been on a bike more than three times in your life."

"I've ridden enough," said Lu. "Besides, if we don't get the prize money, we'll lose the farm."

Lu knew she had to try. But deep down she was sure she didn't have a chance. That's why she was so surprised when Big Mac appeared one night.

"Stick with it," Big Mac said in the dream. "Stay in till the end, no matter what. Uncle Sam will pull you through."

Now Lu didn't have an Uncle Sam —except the U.S. Government, of course. And she couldn't see what they had to do with it. That's why it all seemed so crazy to her.

Speed Domiter was the favorite to win. And he was bragging to everyone how Big Mac had come to him. Lu didn't say anything. Maybe he was right. Her dream was dumb, anyway.

Sure enough, she was eating dust from the start. Everybody passed her along Marsh Creek Road. At the bottom of Lizard Mountain she was dead last.

No one knows how she managed to get up the mountain. And it was a miracle that she got down through Suicide Gulch. But somehow she made it. Then here comes Speed Domiter, starting his third lap, while she was only on her second.

As a joke, Speed ran her off the road into a ditch. You never saw a person as mad as Lu was. She got back on her bike and chased after Speed. She chased him for three more laps. She didn't catch him. But she didn't fall further behind either.

Speed was the favorite to win.

Then it started to rain. It came on all of a sudden. The thunder crashed and the lightning crackled. Pretty soon it was a real "gully-washer" — the kind you only get in that part of Kentucky. It didn't take long for the roads to turn to mud.

Joe King's bike had good tires and a good engine. A little rain and mud wouldn't hurt it. Lu skidded all over the place but she hung on.

Pretty soon she passed Duke Morgan on the way up Lizard Mountain. He had stalled and couldn't get started again. Then she passed two more bikes that had skidded off the road. That's when she started to think she might have a chance.

"Stick with it, Lu." She seemed to hear Big Mac just like in her dream.

By the time she got to the ridge, she had passed more riders. Speed was the only one ahead of her. And she found him at Suicide Gulch. His bike had gone into the gorge. He had jumped off just in time.

"Glory be!" she hollered. "All I got to do is finish. I'm the only one left."

That's when she hit a mud hole and stuck tight. First she got mad. Then she got scared. She was sinking into the mud. It was like quicksand.

"Help!" she called. But who was to hear her in all that rain? The fact is, no one did. It began to look like the end for Lu.

She seemed to hear Big Mac again. *"Uncle Sam will pull you through."*

"Well, if he's going to do it," she said, "he'd better hurry up."

The only thing around was a poor old mule lost in the storm. Luckily, as it passed by, Lu was able to grab its tail.

"Pull, mule!" she hollered.

The old mule was surprised, but he pulled her out. Then she got him to pull out the motorcycle too. The race wasn't over yet. All she had to do was roll down the mountain.

It was raining so hard everyone had gone home. There was just one old man still outside. He was looking for something. His name was Jake Skinner. He had a small farm up on Lizard Mountain.

"You just finish the race?" he asked her.

"Yeah," Lu said.

"I guess you win then," Jake said. "Nobody else has come down." All the time he kept looking up and down the road.

"What are you looking for, Jake?" Lu asked.

"I'm looking for my mule—Uncle Sam," Jake said. "He wandered off in the storm."

"Well, I'll be dangled," Lu said. "Uncle Sam did pull me through, just like Big Mac said."

"What did you say, Lu?" the old man asked.

"I said Uncle Sam will pull through OK."

"Sure he will," Jake said. "He always does."

Order on the Court

Allen Farber was very good at his work. A local newspaper called him "very professional." His business cards read:

T*H*E G*R*E*A*T F*A*R*B*E*R

Master Magician

Reasonable rates for parties, weddings, etc.

Allen wasn't very well liked at school, though. People said he had no interest in anything but his magic. Indeed, he had very little interest in things happening at Defoe High School. The reason was he just didn't have the time. When he wasn't putting on shows, he was practicing. What people said didn't bother him much.

At least it didn't bother him till he met Alice. Alice was a cheerleader. She was very gung-ho on school sports. She never missed a team event. Even the fencing team could count on hearing her chant:

> Deee-foe, Deee-foe,
> You know, you know—
> Let's go!
> Team! Team! Team!

"How can we be friends?" she asked Allen. "We have nothing in common.

The school means everything to me. It means nothing to you."

"But I like the school," Allen objected. "It's just I don't have time. My magic . . ."

"That's just it," Alice said. "It's always your magic. How many card tricks can a person watch?"

"But Alice—I love you!" Allen blurted it out. He hadn't meant to.

Alice caught her breath. She wasn't expecting that. But she made the most of it. "Prove it, then," she said. "Do something for the school *and* for me."

Allen sighed. He felt he had set the trap himself and she was about to spring it. "Name it," he said. "I'll do it."

"The basketball team is in a slump," Alice said. "The team needs our support. But we can't get the crowds. Maybe the Great Farber can bring out a few more fans."

"You want me to do this . . . for

free?" Allen choked on the words. He never put on free shows.

"For free," Alice said.

Allen was too much in love to object. "Only for you, Alice," he said. "Only for you."

*   *   *

Allen was a little late arriving at the gym. Alice and her friends were already busy trying to warm up the small crowd:

> Deee-foe, Deee-foe,
> You know, you know —
> Let's go!
> Team! Team! Team!

They did splits two feet in the air. Angela did a back flip. Alice, Angela, and Wanda did a triple Johnny-on-the-pony. And they finished with a shuffle-off-to-Buffalo. The Defoe rooters didn't even clap.

Allen was busy setting up his sign, T*H*E G*R*E*A*T F*A*R*B*E*R, when Alice came over.

"Do something, Allen," she pleaded. "This is the deadest crowd I ever saw."

"Leave it to the Great Farber," Allen said.

Just then the Eton Tigers ran onto the court. They were led by their coach. He was small and fat. Allen ran to meet him.

"What have you got under the sweatshirt, coach?" Allen shouted so all could hear. He lifted the coach's shirt and pulled out a duck.

At first there was a shocked silence. Then the crowd roared.

"Get this joker out of here!" the coach screamed.

"I go," said the Great Farber. "But I shall return!" He marched off the court and the Tigers began their warm-up.

The biggest man on the Tigers was High Pockets Gordon—six feet four. High Pockets was doing lay-ups when he noticed a small rabbit hopping behind him. Everyone else noticed, too. The crowd roared. The warm-up stopped dead because the players were laughing so hard.

Then the Defoe Blue Devils came on the court. Lights flashed. Rockets shot across the gym. The lights went out and a ghostly blue devil rose in the air. The crowd went wild. The cheerleaders stopped in mid-chant. The Great Farber bowed to the applause.

The Tigers got off to a fast start. They scored two quick ones—4-0. But the next time they set up a shot, the

High Pockets Gordon noticed a small rabbit on the court.

basket turned upside down. A miss!

The Blue Devils worked the ball down court. The Tiger defense was tight. Whitey Reed was looking for an opening. But Lou Tenio of the Tigers was sticking to him like glue.

Suddenly Tenio felt a fly buzzing on his nose. He brushed at it. Then he swatted his nose. That's all the opening Whitey needed. Score!

At half-time the score was 48-16, Blue Devils. The Tigers' coach was screaming "Foul!" at the referee.

"I protest," he shouted. "We play under protest!" Suddenly a stream of shredded paper seemed to pour out of his mouth.

Alice took the Great Farber aside. "I think you better cool it, Allen," she said. "They're getting pretty hot."

"But you said I should help the team," Allen cried.

"I don't care. You're ruining the game," Alice said.

"Maybe I'm ruining the game for the cheerleaders," replied Allen.

This made Alice mad. She boiled over. "Now you listen to me, voodoo man," she said. "You may think you're great. I think you're a twerp. Now get out of this gym. And get out of my life!"

Allen was crushed. But he wouldn't leave. Four minutes into the second half the referee blew his whistle. The play stopped while he picked a quarter off the floor. No sooner did they start playing again than High Pockets Gordon found another quarter. Soon both teams were picking up quarters. They seemed to appear from nowhere.

A guard was sent to get rid of the Great Farber. But the crowd was chanting *We want Farber! We want Farber!* They booed the guard. They

"The Great Farber."

booed the officials. They booed the teams. It looked like the beginning of a riot.

The Great Farber stayed and the crowd cheered. And he left the teams pretty much alone after that. It was just that whenever Defoe scored, a flock of doves seemed to fly out of the basket. The crowd loved it. Alice and Wanda and Angela just sat on their hands.

The Blue Devils won that night 76-68. And, at the end of the game, Allen walked over to Alice. He wanted to try to make up if he could.

"Hey Alice," he said. "I think I like basketball. See you next week, OK?"

Alice said, "Hmmmph!" She put her nose in the air and stomped off. People were laughing. She turned to look. There was nothing to see. She didn't notice the sign pinned to her back. It said:

T*H*E G*R*E*A*T F*A*R*B*E*R

Master Magician

Reasonable rates for parties, weddings, etc.

The Great Farber bowed to the roar of the crowd.

Elmo's Grand Slam

The Bronx Cheers were having a bad season. They had won only 5 games out of 23. Tom O'Toole figured the average. It was a lousy .217. Tom was the manager that year.

It happens that Tom was a grouch when things were going well. When things were bad you couldn't even talk to him. He'd bite your head off. After a two-week losing streak, he was a terror.

"I would be better off in the little leagues!" he shouted. "Those kids *try* to play baseball at least. You bums don't even try!"

The team sulked in silence.

"Hugger!"

Pete Hugger looked up when his name was called.

"Hugger the Slugger," his manager sneered at him. "My ace clean-up batter." Tom wagged an angry finger. "One more game without a hit and that's just what you'll do. Clean up! You'll be cleaning up the bleachers, that's what you'll do."

"Walker!"

Ed Walker shifted on the bench. He was the star pitcher, but he hadn't won a game.

"If you're blind, you poor man, tell me. I'll get you a seeing-eye dog. If you aren't blind, come with me. I want to show you what home plate looks like. Maybe you can find it next time by yourself."

One by one the manager lashed the players with his bitter tongue.

"I'll do it," he said. "I'll bring in a little-leaguer. He'll make monkeys out of you apes!"

Tom O'Toole was a man of his word. He had decided he would try to shame his team into winning. So when they faced the Greenpoint Giants there was a new man in the line-up. He was listed as Elmo Puffin.

Elmo was no more than four feet tall. It was hard to tell how old he was. He may have been no more than nine or ten. Or, he could have been a small teen-ager. Pete Hugger said he thought Elmo was a midget. I think he was just a kid from the little leagues.

Anyhow, the Cheers did try as hard as they could that day. You have to give them credit. But at the bottom of the ninth they were down 3-0. Tom O'Toole was steaming.

The first man up struck out. Tom buried his face in his hands. The second man popped out to the shortstop. Tom groaned. He looked over at Elmo who was blowing bubbles. "Should I do it?" he asked himself.

Then there was the crack of bat on ball. Ron Smith got a base hit. Fred Adams walked. Denny Bean walked. The bases were loaded. Suddenly there was hope!

Tom O'Toole was on his feet now. It was Pete Hugger's turn to bat. Tom shouted:

"Pinch hitter! Elmo Puffin batting for Hugger."

The players gasped. They didn't think Tom would do it. They figured his mind had snapped. Two out, bases loaded, and he puts in a little kid for the great Hugger Slugger.

Elmo grabbed his little-league bat and trotted onto the field. The crowd started to laugh. They thought it was a gag. The plate umpire wanted to know what was going on. The Cheers got to their feet and began shouting at Tom.

Tom stood firm. "He's in the line-up and I say he bats!"

When things quieted down Elmo was at the plate. His little bat was on his shoulder. He was ready. He crouched and took a few practice swings. That's when the Giants' pitcher saw the method in Tom's madness.

How could he pitch to someone that small? He couldn't. It would be a sure walk. It would walk in a run and keep the Cheers alive. Then a lucky hit could tie the game, or even win it.

The pitcher talked to the catcher. Both of them talked to the pitching coach. Then they all talked to the

Elmo was ready.

Giants' manager. Pretty soon the whole team was talking, spitting, and scratching dirt. Each one had a different idea. None of the ideas were any good. They checked with the umpire. "It's legal," he said.

"Well, nothing for it but to try then," said the manager.

The plate umpire shouted, "Play ball!"

The first pitch was a foot and a half over Elmo's head. "Ball one!" the umpire called.

The catcher signaled for a low pitch. It went in the dirt. "Ball two!" Elmo just stood there smiling. And that's all he was supposed to do. Tom had told him to just wait out a walk.

The pitcher was desperate. He tried pitching underhand. This came close but it was still over Elmo's head. "Ball three!"

The catcher had an idea. He would

try an old trick. He signaled for a slow, easy pitch. As the ball sailed over the plate he shouted, "Swing, kid!"

Elmo swung. Instead of missing, though, his little bat hit the ball. The ball rolled about five feet into fair territory. Elmo looked surprised. Then he took off for first as fast as his little legs could carry him. It wasn't very fast.

The catcher and pitcher both dashed after the ball. The catcher got there first and fumbled it. It squirted out toward second base. Elmo was almost to first now. Ron Smith scored from third.

The second baseman and the shortstop met head-on as they chased the slow-rolling ball. Elmo rounded first and made it to second. He was tired and out of breath now. Fred Adams scored.

The whole Giant team was looking for the ball. They finally found it under the shortstop, who had been knocked

*The second baseman and the shortstop met
head-on.*

cold. Elmo was on third and Denny Bean scored. Elmo was so tired he could hardly move. But the third-base coach shoved him toward home.

The Giants' catcher grabbed the ball and raced Elmo for home. Elmo was ready to collapse. But in his hurry, the catcher didn't see Elmo's little bat lying there. He tripped on it and fell — inches short of tagging Elmo. Elmo fell gasping on home plate. It was a grand-slam homer!

That broke the Cheers' losing streak. Tom O'Toole had made his point. He would keep Elmo, he decided, as a threat to his players.

But in the excitement, Elmo Puffin had disappeared. He quit baseball. It was too tough for him. The word is — and I don't know if it's true — that Elmo signed on as a place kicker for a major-league football team instead.

Hot-Dog Skier

"HOT DAWG!" The cry echoed off the mountain.

A skier shoved off and began his run. As he went, he spun gracefully on one ski. Then he leaped into the air. When he landed, he was skiing backwards!

The next skier started downhill in a crouch. He came to a small jump and soared into the air. He did a back-flip and continued on his way as if nothing had happened.

This was "hot-dog" skiing. The skiers weren't just fast. They were dancers and acrobats. Roger Rogers stared glumly at the athletes. His turn would come. And he knew he would fall flat on his face.

"I'll be lucky if I don't break my neck," he mumbled.

"*Ba-a-a-a-a*," the friend at his side said. He looked worried and waggled his big horns from side to side.

Roger's friend was Rod. At this moment, Rod seemed to be the only friend Roger had in the world. And he was just an old Rocky Mountain sheep. He was a ram, to be exact, with heavy spiralled horns. Roger had found him high in the mountains one summer. Rod was just a baby at the time. For some reason, Rod's mother had left him. Maybe hunters got her. Roger never knew what happened to her.

But Roger took the lamb home and fed him with a baby bottle. The animal started following him around like a dog. Rod probably thought Roger was his mother. Now, wherever Roger was, Rod was there, too.

"Poor Pop," Roger said. "He'll really be disappointed with me this time."

"*Ba-a-a-a-a,*" Rod agreed.

Roger's father was Speed Rogers. He had been a world champion skier when he was young. He was still famous now, ten years after he retired from competition. And he drew big crowds to his ski resort. He liked to brag how his son, Roger, would be even better than he was.

The trouble was, Roger just wasn't very good. He could ski well enough. "Better than your average guy," Roger's father would say. But that wasn't what he wanted. Roger's father wanted a champion.

That meant expensive teachers. And Speed got the best for his son. But it didn't do much good.

"Let's face it, Pop," Roger said. "I'm no champion. I never will be."

"Sure you will," his father said. "You're *my* son, aren't you? You're just not trying. You *work* at it, boy. You'll get there."

Roger decided it was time to tell his father that he had another ambition. He wanted to be a dancer. He had taken dance lessons at school, and he was good at it. He was *very* good, his teacher had said. "Keep it up, Roger, and you could be great. A star!"

Roger knew his father wouldn't be pleased. So he just hadn't told him. But, finally, he felt the time had come to tell him.

"Pop," Roger said, "I don't want to

He sensed the danger and stepped in front of Roger.

be a great skier. I want to be a dancer."

His father's face fell. He looked as if someone had slapped him. Then his face got red. "A *what?*" he yelled.

"A dancer," Roger said.

Speed Rogers moved to hit his son. And he would have, too, except for Rod. Rod was with Roger, as he always was. He sensed the danger and stepped in front of Roger. He put his head down and pawed the floor. Roger's father stepped back. There was just no way he could get around those horns. He fell heavily into a chair. "A dancer," he said. "Speed Rogers' son wants to be a dancer."

"That's about it, Pop," Roger said. "I'm sorry."

He petted the sheep to calm him. "It's all right, Rod," he said. "Nobody is going to hurt us."

Suddenly, Roger's father smiled. Then he laughed. "Of course!" he shouted. "I should have known. I should have thought of it myself." He jumped up and slapped his son on the back. The sheep got worried and nervous. "*Ba-a-a-a-a,*" he said. He wanted Mr. Rogers to know he was there and watching.

"Gee, Pop," Roger said. "I'm glad you understand. I thought you'd be angry, and . . . ."

"Angry? Why should I be angry? My son will be the world's greatest hot-dog skier! Why, hot-dog skiing is just like dancing. It's acrobatic dancing on the slopes. The only difference is, you have skis on."

Roger was tired of arguing. He just shook his head and left. Outside he said to Rod, "He wants me to be a hot-dog skier now. OK, I'll be a hot-dog skier. I might as well. We've all got to go sometime."

Rod shook his head. He didn't like the idea.

But that's what Roger was doing up on the mountain. He was waiting his turn to hot-dog it.

"I'll be lucky if I don't break my neck," he said to Rod again.

Rod stepped between Roger and the long downhill slope. "That's OK for mountain sheep," he seemed to be saying. "But you're not a sheep. You're not even a good skier." At any rate, the sheep seemed to understand the danger.

"*Roger Rogers.*" The name boomed over the loudspeakers. The crowd grew silent. This was the son of the great Speed Rogers. Would there be a new champion today?

The ram caught Roger full in the seat of his pants.

"So long, Rod," Roger said. He took the sheep's big horns in his hands and kissed the animal's head. "Take care of yourself," he whispered. Then he stepped to the starting gate.

Roger started off in a deep crouch. Then he heard a shout. "*Look out! Somebody stop him!*" Roger turned his head just in time to see Rod charging at him. His head was down like a battering-ram.

"Rod! Stop!" Roger shouted. But the animal kept coming.

"*Wham!*" The ram caught Roger full in the seat of his pants. Roger did a double back-flip into the air. Somehow, he managed to land on his skis. But he was pointing uphill and sliding backwards. He was out of control. And Rod was coming right after him.

"*Wham!*" The sheep hit again. Roger spun through the air a second time. This time, he landed on Rod's back. He straddled the sheep like a cowboy on a bucking bronco.

By this time, they were at the ski jump. Rod had lost his footing when Roger landed on him. And they went sailing off into space together.

The crowd went wild. "A flying goat!" someone screamed. "What a hot-dogger!" someone else shouted. They cheered themselves hoarse.

Speed Rogers was watching. "Why, the old son of a gun," he said in amazement. "Will you look what that boy of mine cooked up for the show!" Even though he saw it, he could hardly believe it.

When they hit the slope again, Roger had a hold on Rod's horns. They tumbled over and over together in the snow. The last tumble brought Roger upright. And Rod was perched on his shoulders. And that is exactly how they crossed the finish line.

The judges didn't take long to decide on a winner. Roger had topped them all. No one had ever seen a hot-dog ski performance like that. And no one ever expected to see another.

The prize was a gold-plated hot dog with a little pair of skis on it. Roger's father was as proud as he could be. "That's my boy..." he started to say. But he never finished. Roger had shoved the gold-plated hot dog into his father's mouth. And off he went to become a dancer.